'It's like gadgets in shops. You buy a gadget and you develop an affection for it... but all of a sudden there are newer and better gadgets in the shops. More up-to-date models'

WILLIAM TREVOR
Born 24 May 1928, Mitchelstown, Cork, Ireland

'The Mark-2 Wife' first published in book form in *The Ballroom of Romance and Other Stories*, 1972; 'The Time of Year' first published in book form in *Beyond the Pale*, 1981; 'Cheating at Canasta' first published in book form in *Cheating at Canasta*, 2007.

ALSO PUBLISHED BY PENGUIN BOOKS
The Children of Dynmouth · *Fools of Fortune* · *Two Lives* · *Felicia's Journey* · *After Rain* · *The Hill Bachelors* · *The Story of Lucy Gault* · *A Bit on the Side* · *Cheating at Canasta* · *Collected Stories, Volumes 1 and 2* · *Love and Summer*

WILLIAM TREVOR

The Mark-2 Wife

PENGUIN BOOKS

PENGUIN CLASSICS

Published by the Penguin Group

Penguin Books Ltd, 80 Strand, London WC2R ORL, England

Penguin Group (USA) Inc., 375 Hudson Street, New York, New York 10014, USA

Penguin Group (Canada), 90 Eglinton Avenue East, Suite 700, Toronto, Ontario,
Canada M4P 2Y3 (a division of Pearson Penguin Canada Inc.)

Penguin Ireland, 25 St Stephen's Green, Dublin 2, Ireland (a division of Penguin Books Ltd)

Penguin Group (Australia), 250 Camberwell Road, Camberwell, Victoria 3124, Australia
(a division of Pearson Australia Group Pty Ltd)

Penguin Books India Pvt Ltd, 11 Community Centre, Panchsheel Park,
New Delhi – 110 017, India

Penguin Group (NZ), 67 Apollo Drive, Rosedale, North Shore 0632, New Zealand
(a division of Pearson New Zealand Ltd)

Penguin Books (South Africa) (Pty) Ltd, 24 Sturdee Avenue, Rosebank, Johannesburg 2196,
South Africa

Penguin Books Ltd, Registered Offices: 80 Strand, London WC2R ORL, England

www.penguin.com

Selected from *Collected Stories, Volumes 1 and 2*, published by Penguin Books 2009
This edition published in Penguin Classics 2011

1

Typeset by Jouve (UK), Milton Keynes
Printed in England by Clays Ltd, St Ives plc

ISBN: 978-0-141-19624-4

www.greenpenguin.co.uk

est

Contents

The Mark-2 Wife

Standing alone at the Lowhrs' party, Anna Mackintosh thought about her husband Edward, establishing him clearly for this purpose in her mind's eye. He was a thin man, forty-one years of age, with fair hair that was often untidy. In the seventeen years they'd been married he had changed very little: he was still nervous with other people, and smiled in the same abashed way, and his face was still almost boyish. She believed she had failed him because he had wished for children and she had not been able to supply any. She had, over the years, developed a nervous condition about this fact and in the end, quite some time ago now, she had consulted a psychiatrist, a Dr Abbatt, at Edward's pleading.

In the Lowhrs' rich drawing-room, its walls and ceiling gleaming with a metallic surface of ersatz gold, Anna listened to dance music coming from a tape-recorder and continued to think about her husband. In a moment he would be at the party too, since they had agreed to meet there, although by now it was three-quarters of an hour later than the time he had stipulated. The Lowhrs were people he knew in a business way, and he had said he thought it wise that he and Anna should attend this gathering of theirs. She had never met them before, which made it more difficult for her, having to wait about, not knowing a soul in the room. When she thought about it she felt hard done by, for although Edward was kind to her and always had been, it was far from considerate to be as late as this. Because of her nervous condition she felt afraid and had developed a sickness in her stomach. She looked at her watch and sighed.

People arrived, some of them kissing the Lowhrs, others nodding and smiling. Two dark-skinned maids carried trays of drinks among the guests, offering them graciously and murmuring thanks when a glass was accepted. 'I'll be there by half past nine,' Edward had said that morning. 'If you don't turn up till ten you won't have to be alone at all.' He had kissed her after that, and had left the house. I'll wear the blue, she thought, for she liked the colour better than any other: it suggested serenity to her, and the idea of serenity, especially as a quality in herself, was something she valued. She had said as much to Dr Abbatt, who had agreed that serenity was something that should be important in her life.

An elderly couple, tall twig-like creatures of seventy-five, a General Ritchie and his wife, observed the lone state of Anna Mackintosh and reacted in different ways. 'That woman seems out of things,' said Mrs Ritchie. 'We should go and talk to her.'

But the General suggested that there was something the matter with this woman who was on her own. 'Now, don't let's get involved,' he rather tetchily begged. 'In any case she doesn't look in the mood for chat.'

His wife shook her head. 'Our name is Ritchie,' she said to Anna, and Anna, who had been looking at the whisky in her glass, lifted her head and saw a thin old woman who was as straight as a needle, and behind her a man who was thin also but who stooped a bit and seemed to be cross. 'He's an old soldier,' said Mrs Ritchie. 'A general that was.'

Strands of white hair trailed across the pale dome of the old man's head. He had sharp eyes, like a terrier's, and a grey moustache. 'It's not a party I care to be at,' he muttered, holding out a bony hand. 'My wife's the one for this.'

Anna said who she was and added that her husband was late and that she didn't know the Lowhrs.

'We thought it might be something like that,' said Mrs Ritchie. 'We don't know anyone either, but at least we have one another to talk to.' The Lowhrs, she added, were an awfully nice, generous couple.

3

'We met them on a train in Switzerland,' the General murmured quietly.

Anna glanced across the crowded room at the people they spoke of. The Lowhrs were wholly different in appearance from the Ritchies. They were small and excessively fat, and they both wore glasses and smiled a lot. Like jolly gnomes, she thought.

'My husband knows them in a business way,' she said. She looked again at her watch: the time was half past ten. There was a silence, and then Mrs Ritchie said:

'They invited us to two other parties in the past. It's very kind, for we don't give parties ourselves any more. We live a quiet sort of life now.' She went on talking, saying among other things that it was pleasant to see the younger set at play. When she stopped, the General added:

'The Lowhrs feel sorry for us, actually.'

'They're very kind,' his wife repeated.

Anna had been aware of a feeling of uneasiness the moment she'd entered the golden room, and had Edward been with her she'd have wanted to say that they should turn round and go away again. The uneasiness had increased whenever she'd noted the time, and for some reason these old people for whom the Lowhrs were sorry had added to it even more. She would certainly talk this over with Dr Abbatt, she decided, and then, quite absurdly, she felt an urge to telephone Dr Abbatt and tell him at once about the feeling she had. She closed her eyes, thinking that she would keep them like that for only the slightest moment so that the Ritchies wouldn't notice and think it odd. While they were still closed she heard Mrs Ritchie say:

'Are you all right, Mrs Mackintosh?'

She opened her eyes and saw that General Ritchie and his wife were examining her face with interest. She imagined them wondering about her, a woman of forty whose husband was an hour late. They'd be thinking, she thought, that the absent husband didn't have much of a feeling for his wife to be as careless as that. And yet, they'd probably think, he must have had a feeling for her once since he had married her in the first place.

'It's just,' said Mrs Ritchie, 'that I had the notion you were going to faint.'

The voice of Petula Clark came powerfully from the tape-recorder. At one end of the room people were beginning to dance in a casual way, some still holding their glasses in their hands.

'The heat could have affected you,' said the General, bending forward so that his words would reach her.

Anna shook her head. She tried to smile, but the smile failed to materialize. She said:

5

'I never faint, actually.'

She could feel a part of herself attempting to bar from her mind the entry of unwelcome thoughts. Hastily she said, unable to think of anything better:

'My husband's really frightfully late.'

'You know,' said General Ritchie, 'it seems to me we met your husband here.' He turned to his wife. 'A fair-haired man – he said his name was Mackintosh. Is your husband fair, Mrs Mackintosh?'

'Of course,' cried Mrs Ritchie. 'Awfully nice.'

Anna said that Edward was fair. Mrs Ritchie smiled at her husband and handed him her empty glass. He reached out for Anna's. She said:

'Whisky, please. By itself.'

'He's probably held up in bloody traffic,' said the General before moving off.

'Yes, probably that,' Mrs Ritchie said. 'I do remember him well, you know.'

'Edward did come here before. I had a cold.'

'Completely charming. We said so afterwards.'

One of the dark-skinned maids paused with a tray of drinks. Mrs Ritchie explained that her husband was fetching some. 'Thank you, madam,' said the dark-skinned maid, and the General returned.

'It isn't the traffic,' Anna said rather suddenly and loudly. 'Edward's not held up like that at all.'

The Ritchies sipped their drinks. They can sense I'm going to be a nuisance, Anna thought. 'I'm afraid it'll be boring,' he had said. 'We'll slip away at eleven and have dinner in Charlotte Street.' She heard him saying it now, quite distinctly. She saw him smiling at her.

'I get nervous about things,' she said to the Ritchies. 'I worry unnecessarily. I try not to.'

Mrs Ritchie inclined her head in a sympathetic manner; the General coughed. There was a silence and then Mrs Ritchie spoke about episodes in their past. Anna looked at her watch and saw that it was five to eleven. 'Oh God,' she said.

The Ritchies asked her again if she was all right. She began to say she was but she faltered before the sentence was complete, and in that moment she gave up the struggle. What was the point, she thought, of exhausting oneself being polite and making idle conversation when all the time one was in a frightful state?

'He's going to be married again,' she said quietly and evenly. 'His Mark-2 wife.'

She felt better at once. The sickness left her stomach; she drank a little whisky and found its harsh taste a comfort.

'Oh, I'm terribly sorry,' said Mrs Ritchie.

Anna had often dreamed of the girl. She had seen her, dressed all in purple, with slim hips and a purple bow in her black hair. She had seen the two of them together in a speedboat, the beautiful young creature laughing her head off like a figure in an advertisement. She had talked for many hours to Dr Abbatt about her, and Dr Abbatt had made the point that the girl was simply an obsession. 'It's just a little nonsense,' he had said to her kindly, more than once. Anna knew in her calmer moments that it was just a little nonsense, for Edward was always kind and had never ceased to say he loved her. But in bad moments she argued against that conclusion, reminding herself that other kind men who said they loved their wives often made off with something new. Her own marriage being childless would make the whole operation simpler.

'I hadn't thought it would happen at a party,' Anna said to the Ritchies. 'Edward has always been decent and considerate. I imagined he would tell me quietly at home, and comfort me. I imagined he would be decent to the end.'

'You and your husband are not yet separated then?' Mrs Ritchie inquired.

'This is the way it is happening,' Anna repeated. 'D'you understand? Edward is delayed by his Mark-2 wife because she insists on delaying him. She's demanding that he should make his decision and afterwards that he and she should come to tell me, so that I won't

have to wait any more. You understand,' she repeated,
looking closely from one face to the other, 'that this
isn't Edward's doing?'

'But, Mrs Mackintosh –'

'I have a woman's intuition about it. I have felt my
woman's intuition at work since the moment I entered
this room. I know precisely what's going to happen.'

Often, ever since the obsession had begun, she had
wondered if she had any rights at all. Had she rights in
the matter, she had asked herself, since she was running
to fat and could supply no children? The girl would
repeatedly give birth and everyone would be happy,
for birth was a happy business. She had suggested to
Dr Abbatt that she probably hadn't any rights, and for
once he had spoken to her sternly. She said it now to
the Ritchies, because it didn't seem to matter any more
what words were spoken. On other occasions, when
she was at home, Edward had been late and she had sat
and waited for him, pretending it was a natural thing
for him to be late. And when he arrived her fears had
seemed absurd.

'You understand?' she said to the Ritchies.

The Ritchies nodded their thin heads, the General
embarrassed, his wife concerned. They waited for Anna
to speak. She said:

'The Lowhrs will feel sorry for me, as they do for

you. "This poor woman," they'll cry, "left in the lurch at our party! What a ghastly thing!" I should go home, you know, but I haven't even the courage for that.'

'Could we help at all?' asked Mrs Ritchie.

'You've been married all this time and not come asunder. Have you had children, Mrs Ritchie?'

Mrs Ritchie replied that she had had two boys and a girl. They were well grown up by now, she explained, and among them had provided her and the General with a dozen grandchildren.

'What did you think of my husband?'

'Charming, Mrs Mackintosh, as I said.'

'Not the sort of man who'd mess a thing like this up? You thought the opposite, I'm sure: that with bad news to break he'd choose the moment elegantly. Once he would have.'

'I don't understand,' protested Mrs Ritchie gently, and the General lent his support to that with a gesture.

'Look at me,' said Anna. 'I've worn well enough. Neither I nor Edward would deny it. A few lines and flushes, fatter and coarser. No one can escape all that. Did you never feel like a change, General?'

'A change?'

'I have to be rational. I have to say that it's no reflection on me. D'you understand that?'

'Of course it's no reflection.'

'It's like gadgets in shops. You buy a gadget and you develop an affection for it, having decided on it in the first place because you thought it was attractive. But all of a sudden there are newer and better gadgets in the shops. More up-to-date models.' She paused. She found a handkerchief and blew her nose. She said:

'You must excuse me: I am not myself tonight.'

'You mustn't get upset. Please don't,' Mrs Ritchie said.

Anna drank all the whisky in her glass and lifted another glass from a passing tray. 'There are too many people in this room,' she complained. 'There's not enough ventilation. It's ideal for tragedy.'

Mrs Ritchie shook her head. She put her hand on Anna's arm. 'Would you like us to go home with you and see you safely in?'

'I have to stay here.'

'Mrs Mackintosh, your husband would never act like that.'

'People in love are cruel. They think of themselves: why should they bother to honour the feelings of a discarded wife?'

'Oh, come now,' said Mrs Ritchie.

At that moment a bald man came up to Anna and took her glass from her hand and led her, without a word, on to the dancing area. As he danced with her, she thought that something else might have happened. Edward was not with anyone, she said to herself: Edward was dead. A telephone had rung in the Lowhrs' house and a voice had said that, *en route* to their party, a man had dropped dead on the pavement. A maid had taken the message and, not quite understanding it, had done nothing about it.

'I think we should definitely go home now,' General Ritchie said to his wife. 'We could be back for *A Book at Bedtime*.'

'We cannot leave her as easily as that. Just look at the poor creature.'

'That woman is utterly no concern of ours.'

'Just look at her.'

The General sighed and swore and did as he was bidden.

'My husband was meant to turn up,' Anna said to the bald man. 'I've just thought he may have died.' She laughed to indicate that she did not really believe this, in case the man became upset. But the man seemed not to be interested. She could feel his lips playing with a strand of her hair. Death, she thought, she could have accepted.

Anna could see the Ritchies watching her. Their faces were grave, but it came to her suddenly that the gravity was artificial. What, after all, was she to them that they should bother? She was a wretched woman at a party, a woman in a state, who was making an unnecessary fuss because her husband was about to give her her marching orders. Had the Ritchies been mocking her, she wondered, he quite directly, she in some special, subtle way of her own?

'Do you know those people I was talking to?' she said to her partner, but with a portion of her hair still in his mouth he made no effort at reply. Passing near to her, she noticed the thick, square fingers of Mr Lowhr embedded in the flesh of his wife's shoulder. The couple danced by, seeing her and smiling, and it seemed to Anna that their smiles were as empty as the Ritchies' sympathy.

'My husband is leaving me for a younger woman,' she said to the bald man, a statement that caused him to shrug. He had pressed himself close to her, his knees on her thighs, forcing her legs this way and that. His hands were low on her body now, advancing on her buttocks. He was eating her hair.

'I'm sorry,' Anna said. 'I'd rather you didn't do that.'

He released her where they stood and smiled agreeably: she could see pieces of her hair on his teeth. He walked away, and she turned and went in the opposite direction.

'We're really most concerned,' said Mrs Ritchie. She

and her husband were standing where Anna had left them, as though waiting for her. General Ritchie held out her glass to her.

'Why should you be concerned? That bald man ate my hair. That's what people do to used-up women like me. They eat your hair and force their bodies on you. You know, General.'

'Certainly, I don't. Not in the least.'

'That man knew all about me. D'you think he'd have taken his liberties if he hadn't? A man like that can guess.'

'Nonsense,' said Mrs Ritchie firmly. She stared hard at Anna, endeavouring to impress upon her the errors in her logic.

'If you want to know, that man's a drunk,' said the General. 'He was far gone when he arrived here and he's more so now.'

'Why are you saying that?' Anna cried shrilly. 'Why are you telling me lies and mocking me?'

'Lies?' demanded the General, snapping the word out. 'Lies?'

'My dear, we're not mocking you,' murmured Mrs Ritchie.

'You and those Lowhrs and everyone else, God knows. The big event at this party is that Edward Mackintosh will reject his wife for another.'

'Oh now, Mrs Mackintosh –'

'Second marriages are often happier, you know. No reason why they shouldn't be.'

'We would like to help if we could,' Mrs Ritchie said.

'Help? In God's name, how can I be helped? How can two elderly strangers help me when my husband gives me up? What kind of help? Would you give me money – an income, say? Or offer me some other husband? Would you come to visit me and talk to me so that I shouldn't be lonely? Or strike down my husband, General, to show your disapproval? Would you scratch out the little girl's eyes for me, Mrs Ritchie? Would you slap her brazen face?'

'We simply thought we might help in some way,' Mrs Ritchie said. 'Just because we're old and pretty useless doesn't mean we can't make an effort.'

'We are all God's creatures, you are saying. We should offer aid to one another at every opportunity, when marriages get broken and decent husbands are made cruel. Hold my hands then, and let us wait for Edward and his Mark-2 wife. Let's all three speak together and tell them what we think.'

She held out her hands, but the Ritchies did not take them.

'We don't mean to mock you, as you seem to think,' the General said. 'I must insist on that, madam.'

'You're mocking me with your talk about helping. The world is not like that. You like to listen to me for my entertainment value: I'm a good bit of gossip for you. I'm a woman going on about her husband and then getting insulted by a man and seeing the Lowhrs smiling over it. Tell your little grandchildren that some time.'

Mrs Ritchie said that the Lowhrs, she was sure, had not smiled at any predicament that Anna had found herself in, and the General impatiently repeated that the man was drunk.

'The Lowhrs smiled,' Anna said, 'and you have mocked me too. Though perhaps you don't even know it.'

As she pushed a passage through the people, she felt the sweat running on her face and her body. There was a fog of smoke in the room by now, and the voices of the people, struggling to be heard above the music, were louder than before. The man she had danced with was sitting in a corner with his shoes off, and a woman in a crimson dress was trying to persuade him to put them on again. At the door of the room she found Mr Lowhr. 'Shall we dance?' he said.

She shook her head, feeling calmer all of a sudden. Mr Lowhr suggested a drink.

'May I telephone?' she said. 'Quietly somewhere?'

'Upstairs,' said Mr Lowhr, smiling immensely at her.

'Up two flights, the door ahead of you: a tiny guest-room. Take a glass with you.'

She nodded, saying she'd like a little whisky.

'Let me give you a tip,' Mr Lowhr said as he poured her some from a nearby bottle. 'Always buy Haig whisky. It's distilled by a special method.'

'You're never going so soon?' said Mrs Lowhr, appearing at her husband's side.

'Just to telephone,' said Mr Lowhr. He held out his hand with the glass of whisky in it. Anna took it, and as she did so she caught a glimpse of the Ritchies watching her from the other end of the room. Her calmness vanished. The Lowhrs, she noticed, were looking at her too, and smiling. She wanted to ask them why they were smiling, but she knew if she did that they'd simply make some polite reply. Instead she said:

'You shouldn't expose your guests to men who eat hair. Even unimportant guests.'

She turned her back on them and passed from the room. She crossed the hall, sensing that she was being watched. 'Mrs Mackintosh,' Mr Lowhr called after her.

His plumpness filled the doorway. He hovered, seeming uncertain about pursuing her. His face was bewildered and apparently upset.

'Has something disagreeable happened?' he said in a low voice across the distance between them.

'You saw. You and your wife thought fit to laugh, Mr Lowhr.'

'I do assure you, Mrs Mackintosh, I've no idea what you're talking about.'

'It's fascinating, I suppose. Your friends the Ritchies find it fascinating too.'

'Look here, Mrs Mackintosh –'

'Oh, don't blame them. They've nothing left but to watch and mock, at an age like that. The point is, there's a lot of hypocrisy going on tonight.' She nodded at Mr Lowhr to emphasize that last remark, and then went swiftly upstairs.

'I imagine the woman's gone off home,' the General said. 'I dare say her husband's drinking in a pub.'

'I worried once,' replied Mrs Ritchie, speaking quietly, for she didn't wish the confidence to be heard by others. 'That female, Mrs Flyte.'

The General roared with laughter. 'Trixie Flyte,' he shouted. 'Good God, she was a free-for-all!'

'Oh, do be quiet.'

'Dear girl, you didn't ever think –'

'I didn't know what to think, if you want to know.'

Greatly amused, the General seized what he hoped would be his final drink. He placed it behind a green plant on a table. 'Shall we dance one dance,' he said, 'just to amuse them? And then when I've had that drink to revive me we can thankfully make our way.'

But he found himself talking to nobody, for when he had turned from his wife to secrete his drink she had moved away. He followed her to where she was questioning Mrs Lowhr.

'Some little tiff,' Mrs Lowhr was saying as he approached.

'Hardly a tiff,' corrected Mrs Ritchie. 'The woman's terribly upset.' She turned to her husband, obliging him to speak.

'Upset,' he said.

'Oh, there now,' cried Mrs Lowhr, taking each of the Ritchies by an arm. 'Why don't you take the floor and forget it?'

They both of them recognized from her tone that she was thinking the elderly exaggerated things and didn't always understand the ways of marriage in the modern world. The General especially resented the insinuation. He said:

'Has the woman gone away?'

'She's upstairs telephoning. Some silly chap upset her apparently, during a dance. That's all it is, you know.'

'You've got the wrong end of the stick entirely,' said the General angrily, 'and you're trying to say we have.

The woman believes her husband may arrive here with the girl he's chosen as his second wife.'

'But that's ridiculous!' cried Mrs Lowhr with a tinkling laugh.

'It is what the woman thinks,' said the General loudly, 'whether it's ridiculous or not.' More quietly, Mrs Ritchie added:

'She thinks she has a powerful intuition when all it is is a disease.'

'I'm cross with this Mrs Mackintosh for upsetting you two dear people!' cried Mrs Lowhr with a shrillness that matched her roundness and her glasses. 'I really and truly am.'

A big man came up as she spoke and lifted her into his arms, preparatory to dancing with her. 'What could anyone do?' she called back at the Ritchies as the man rotated her away. 'What can you do for a nervy woman like that?'

There was dark wallpaper on the walls of the room: black and brown with little smears of muted yellow. The curtains matched it; so did the bedspread on the low single bed, and the covering on the padded headboard. The carpet ran from wall to wall and was black and thick. There was a narrow wardrobe with a door of padded black leather and brass studs and an ornamental brass handle. The dressing-table and the stool in front of it reflected this general motif in different ways. Two shelves, part of the bed, attached to it on either side of the pillows, served as bedside tables: on each there was a lamp, and on one of them a white telephone.

As Anna closed and locked the door, she felt that in a dream she had been in a dark room in a house where there was a party, waiting for Edward to bring her terrible news. She drank a little whisky and moved towards the telephone. She dialled a number and when a voice answered her call she said:

'Dr Abbatt? It's Anna Mackintosh.'

His voice, as always, was so soft she could hardly hear it. 'Ah, Mrs Mackintosh,' he said.

'I want to talk to you.'

'Of course, Mrs Mackintosh, of course. Tell me now.'

'I'm at a party given by people called Lowhr. Edward was to be here but he didn't turn up. I was all alone and then two old people like scarecrows talked to me. They said their name was Ritchie. And a man ate my hair when we were dancing. The Lowhrs smiled at that.'

'I see. Yes?'

'I'm in a room at the top of the house. I've locked the door.'

'Tell me about the room, Mrs Mackintosh.'

'There's black leather on the wardrobe and the dressing-table. Curtains and things match. Dr Abbatt?'

'Yes?'

'The Ritchies are people who injure other people, I think. Intentionally or unintentionally, it never matters.'

'They are strangers to you, these Ritchies?'

'They attempted to mock me. People know at this party, Dr Abbatt; they sense what's going to happen because of how I look.'

Watching for her to come downstairs, the Ritchies stood in the hall and talked to one another.

'I'm sorry,' said Mrs Ritchie. 'I know it would be nicer to go home.'

'What can we do, old sticks like us? We know not a thing about such women. It's quite absurd.'

'The woman's on my mind, dear. And on yours too. You know it.'

'I think she'll be more on our minds if we come across her again. She'll turn nasty, I'll tell you that.'

'Yes, but it would please me to wait a little.'

'To be insulted,' said the General.

'Oh, do stop being so cross, dear.'

'The woman's a stranger to us. She should regulate

her life and have done with it. She has no right to bother people.'

'She is a human being in great distress. No, don't say anything, please, if it isn't pleasant.'

The General went into a sulk, and at the end of it he said grudgingly:

'Trixie Flyte was nothing.'

'Oh, I know. Trixie Flyte is dead and done for years ago. I didn't worry like this woman if that's what's on your mind.'

'It wasn't,' lied the General. 'The woman worries ridiculously.'

'I think, you know, we may yet be of use to her: I have a feeling about that.'

'For God's sake, leave the feelings to her. We've had enough of that for one day.'

'As I said to her, we're not entirely useless. No one ever can be.'

'You feel you're being attacked again, Mrs Mackintosh. Are you calm? You haven't been drinking too much?'

'A little.'

'I see.'

'I am being replaced by a younger person.'

'You say you're in a bedroom. Is it possible for you to

lie on the bed and talk to me at the same time? Would it be comfortable?'

Anna placed the receiver on the bed and settled herself. She picked it up again and said:

'If he died, there would be a funeral and I'd never forget his kindness to me. I can't do that if he has another wife.'

'We have actually been over this ground,' said Dr Abbatt more softly than ever. 'But we can of course go over it again.'

'Any time, you said.'

'Of course.'

'What has happened is perfectly simple. Edward is with the girl. He is about to arrive here to tell me to clear off. She's insisting on that. It's not Edward, you know.'

'Mrs Mackintosh, I'm going to speak firmly now. We've agreed between us that there's no young girl in your husband's life. You have an obsession, Mrs Mackintosh, about the fact that you have never had children and that men sometimes marry twice –'

'There's such a thing as the Mark-2 wife!' Anna cried. 'You know there is. A girl of nineteen who'll delightedly give birth to Edward's sons.'

'No, no –'

'I had imagined Edward telling me. I had imagined

him pushing back his hair and lighting a cigarette in his untidy way. "I'm terribly sorry," he would say, and leave me nothing to add to that. Instead it's like this: a nightmare.'

'It is not a nightmare, Mrs Mackintosh.'

'This party is a nightmare. People are vultures here.'

'Mrs Mackintosh, I must tell you that I believe you're seeing the people at this party in a most exaggerated light.'

'A man –'

'A man nibbled your hair. Worse things can happen. This is not a nightmare, Mrs Mackintosh. Your husband has been delayed. Husbands are always being delayed. D'you see? You and I and your husband are all together trying to rid you of this perfectly normal obsession you've developed. We mustn't complicate matters, now must we?'

'I didn't run away, Dr Abbatt. I said to myself I mustn't run away from this party. I must wait and face whatever was to happen. You told me to face things.'

'I didn't tell you, my dear. We agreed between us. We talked it out, the difficulty about facing things, and we saw the wisdom of it. Now I want you to go back to the party and wait for your husband.'

'He's more than two hours late.'

'My dear Mrs Mackintosh, an hour or so is absolutely nothing these days. Now listen to me please.'

25

She listened to the soft voice as it reminded her of all that between them they had agreed. Dr Abbatt went over the ground, from the time she had first consulted him to the present moment. He charted her obsession until it seemed once again, as he said, a perfectly normal thing for a woman of forty to have.

After she had said goodbye, Anna sat on the bed feeling very calm. She had read the message behind Dr Abbatt's words: that it was ridiculous, her perpetually going on in this lunatic manner. She had come to a party and in no time at all she'd been behaving in a way that was, she supposed, mildly crazy. It always happened, she knew, and it would as long as the trouble remained: in her mind, when she began to worry, everything became jumbled and unreal, turning her into an impossible person. How could Edward, for heaven's sake, be expected to live with her fears and her suppositions? Edward would crack as others would, tormented by an impossible person. He'd become an alcoholic or he'd have some love affair with a woman just as old as she was, and the irony of that would be too great. She knew, as she sat there, that she couldn't help herself and that as long as she lived with Edward she wouldn't be able to do any better. 'I have lost touch with reality,' she said. 'I shall let him go, as a bird is released. In my state how can I have rights?'

She left the room and slowly descended the stairs. There were framed prints of old motor-cars on the wall and she paused now and again to examine one, emphasizing to herself her own continued calmness. She was thinking that she'd get herself a job. She might even tell Edward that Dr Abbatt had suggested their marriage should end since she wasn't able to live with her thoughts any more. She'd insist on a divorce at once. She didn't mind the thought of it now, because of course it would be different: she was doing what she guessed Dr Abbatt had been willing her to do for quite a long time really: she was taking matters into her own hands, she was acting positively – rejecting, not being rejected herself. Her marriage was ending cleanly and correctly.

She found her coat and thanked the dark-skinned maid who held it for her. Edward was probably at the party by now, but in the new circumstances that was neither here nor there. She'd go home in a taxi and pack a suitcase and then telephone for another taxi. She'd leave a note for Edward and go to a hotel, without telling him where.

'Good-night,' she said to the maid. She stepped towards the hall door as the maid opened it for her, and as she did so she felt a hand touch her shoulder. 'No, Edward,' she said. 'I must go now.' But when she turned she saw that the hand belonged to Mrs Ritchie. Behind

27

her, looking tired, stood the General. For a moment there was a silence. Then Anna, speaking to both of them, said:

'I'm extremely sorry. Please forgive me.'

'We were worried about you,' said Mrs Ritchie. 'Will you be all right, my dear?'

'The fear is worse than the reality, Mrs Ritchie. I can no longer live with the fear.'

'We understand.'

'It's strange,' Anna said, passing through the doorway and standing at the top of the steps that led to the street. 'Strange, coming to a party like this, given by people I didn't know and meeting you and being so rude. Please don't tell me if my husband is here or not. It doesn't concern me now. I'm quite calm.'

The Ritchies watched her descend the steps and call out to a passing taxi-cab. They watched the taxi drive away.

'Calm!' said General Ritchie.

'She's still in a state, poor thing,' agreed his wife. 'I do feel sorry.'

They stood on the steps of the Lowhrs' house, thinking about the brief glance they had had of another person's life, bewildered by it and saddened, for they themselves, though often edgy on the surface, had had a happy marriage.

'At least she's standing on her own feet now,' Mrs Ritchie said. 'I think it'll save her.'

A taxi drew up at the house and the Ritchies watched it, thinking for a moment that Anna Mackintosh, weak in her resolve, had returned in search of her husband. But it was a man who emerged and ran up the steps in a manner which suggested that, like the man who had earlier misbehaved on the dance-floor, he was not entirely sober. He passed the Ritchies and entered the house. 'That is Edward Mackintosh,' said Mrs Ritchie.

The girl who was paying the taxi-driver paused in what she was doing to see where her companion had dashed away to and observed two thin figures staring at her from the lighted doorway, murmuring to one another.

'Cruel,' said the General. 'The woman said so: we must give her that.'

'He's a kind man,' replied Mrs Ritchie. 'He'll listen to us.'

'To us, for heaven's sake?'

'We have a thing to do, as I said we might have.'

'The woman has gone. I'm not saying I'm not sorry for her –'

'And who shall ask for mercy for the woman, since she cannot ask herself? There is a little to be saved, you know: she has made a gesture, poor thing. It must be honoured.'

'My dear, we don't know these people; we met the woman quite in passing.'

The girl came up the steps, settling her purse into its right place in her handbag. She smiled at the Ritchies, and they thought that the smile had a hint of triumph about it, as though it was her first smile since the victory that Anna Mackintosh had said some girl was winning that night.

'Even if he'd listen,' muttered the General when the girl had passed by, 'I doubt that she would.'

'It's just that a little time should be allowed to go by,' his wife reminded him. 'That's all that's required. Until the woman's found her feet again and feels she has a voice in her own life.'

'We're interfering,' said the General, and his wife said nothing. They looked at one another, remembering vividly the dread in Anna Mackintosh's face and the confusion that all her conversation had revealed.

The General shook his head. 'We are hardly the happiest choice,' he said, in a gentler mood at last, 'but I dare say we must try.'

He closed the door of the house and they paused for a moment in the hall, talking again of the woman who had told them her troubles. They drew a little strength from that, and felt armed to face once more the Lowhrs' noisy party. Together they moved towards it and through it, in search of a man they had met once before on a similar occasion. 'We are sorry for interfering,' they would quietly say; and making it seem as natural as they could, they would ask him to honour, above all else and in spite of love, the gesture of a woman who no longer interested him.

'A tall order,' protested the General, pausing in his forward motion, doubtful again.

'When the wrong people do things,' replied his wife, 'it sometimes works.' She pulled him on until they stood before Edward Mackintosh and the girl he'd chosen as his Mark-2 wife. They smiled at Edward Mackintosh and shook hands with him, and then there was a silence before the General said that it was odd, in a way, what they had to request.

The Time of Year

All that autumn, when they were both fourteen, they had talked about their Christmas swim. She'd had the idea: that on Christmas morning when everyone was still asleep they would meet by the boats on the strand at Ballyquin and afterwards quite casually say that they had been for a swim on Christmas Day. Whenever they met during that stormy October and November they wondered how fine the day might be, how cold or wet, and if the sea could possibly be frozen. They walked together on the cliffs, looking down at the breaking waves of the Atlantic, shivering in anticipation. They walked through the misty dusk of the town, lingering over the first signs of Christmas in the shops: coloured lights strung up, holly and Christmas trees and tinsel. They wondered if people guessed about them. They didn't want them to, they wanted it to be a secret. People would laugh because they were children. They were in love that autumn.

Six years later Valerie still remembered, poignantly, in November. Dublin, so different from Ballyquin, stirred up the past as autumn drifted into winter and winds bustled around the grey buildings of Trinity College, where she was now a student. The city's trees were bleakly bare, it seemed to Valerie; there was sadness, even, on the lawns of her hall of residence, scattered with finished leaves. In her small room, preparing herself one Friday evening for the Skullys' end-of-term party, she sensed quite easily the Christmas chill of the sea, the chilliness creeping slowly over her calves and knees. She paused with the memory, gazing at herself in the looking-glass attached to the inside of her cupboard door. She was a tall girl, standing now in a white silk petticoat, with a thin face and thin long fingers and an almost classical nose. Her black hair was straight, falling to her shoulders. She was pretty when she smiled and she did so at her reflection, endeavouring to overcome the melancholy that visited her at this time of year. She turned away and picked up a green corduroy dress which she had laid out on her bed. She was going to be late if she dawdled like this.

The parties given by Professor and Mrs Skully were renowned neither for the entertainment they provided nor for their elegance. They were, unfortunately, difficult to avoid, the Professor being persistent in the face of repeated excuses – a persistence it was deemed unwise to strain.

Bidden for half past seven, his history students came on bicycles, a few in Kilroy's Mini, Ruth Cusper on her motor-cycle, Bewley Joal on foot. Woodward, Whipp and Woolmer-Mills came cheerfully, being kindred spirits of the Professor's and in no way dismayed by the immediate prospect. Others were apprehensive or cross, trying not to let it show as smilingly they entered the Skullys' house in Rathgar.

'How very nice!' Mrs Skully murmured in a familiar manner in the hall. 'How jolly good of you to come.'

The hall was not yet decorated for Christmas, but the Professor had found the remains of last year's crackers and had stuck half a dozen behind the heavily framed scenes of Hanover that had been established in the hall since the early days of the Skullys' marriage. The gaudy crêpe paper protruded above the pictures in splurges of green, red and yellow, and cheered up the hall to a small extent. The coloured scarves and overcoats of the history students, already accumulating on the hall-stand, did so more effectively.

In the Skullys' sitting-room the Professor's record-player, old and in some way special, was in its usual place: on a mahogany table in front of the french windows, which were now obscured by brown curtains. Four identical rugs, their colour approximately matching that of the curtains, were precisely arranged on darker brown linoleum. Crimson-seated dining-chairs lined brownish walls.

The Professor's history students lent temporary character to this room, as their coats and scarves did to the hall. Kilroy was plump in a royal-blue suit. The O'Neill sisters' cluster of followers, jostling even now for promises of favours, wore carefully pressed denim or tweed. The O'Neill sisters themselves exuded a raffish, cocktail-time air. They were twins, from Lurgan, both of them blonde and both favouring an excess of eye-shadow, with lipstick that wetly gleamed, the same shade of pink as the trouser-suits that nudgingly hugged the protuberances of their bodies. Not far from where they now held court, the rimless spectacles of Bewley Joal had a busy look in the room's harsh light; the complexion of Yvonne Smith was displayed to disadvantage. So was the troublesome fair hair of Honor Hitchcock, who was engaged to a student known as the Reverend because of his declared intention one day to claim the title. Cosily in a corner she linked her arm with his, both of them seeming middle-aged before their time, inmates already of a draughty rectory in Co. Cork or Clare. 'I'll be the first,' Ruth Cusper vowed, 'to visit you in your parish. Wherever it is.' Ruth Cusper was a statuesque English girl, not yet divested of her motor-cycling gear.

The colours worn by the girls, and the denim and tweed, and the royal blue of Kilroy, contrasted sharply with the uncared-for garb of Woodward, Whipp and Woolmer-Mills, all of whom were expected to take Firsts. Stained and frayed, these three hung together without speaking, Woodward very tall, giving the impression of an etiolated newt, Whipp small, his glasses repaired with Sellotape, Woolmer-Mills for ever launching himself back and forth on the balls of his feet.

In a pocket of Kilroy's suit there was a miniature bottle of vodka, for only tea and what the Professor described as 'cup' were served in the course of the evening. Kilroy fingered it, smiling across the room at the Professor, endeavouring to give the impression that he was delighted to be present. He was a student who was fearful of academic failure, his terror being that he would not get a Third: he had set his sights on a Third, well aware that to have set them higher would not be wise. He brought his little bottles of vodka to the Professor's parties as an act of bravado, a gesture designed to display jauntiness, to show that he could take a chance. But the chances he took with his vodka were not great.

Bewley Joal, who would end up with a respectable Second, was laying down the law to Yvonne Smith, who would be grateful to end up with anything at all. Her natural urge to chatter was stifled, for no one could get a word in when the clanking voice of Bewley Joal was in full flow. 'Oh, it's far more than just a solution, dear girl,' he breezily pronounced, speaking of Moral Rearmament. Yvonne Smith nodded and agreed, trying to say that an aunt of hers thought most highly of Moral Rearmament, that she herself had always been meaning to look into it. But the voice of Bewley Joal cut all her sentences in half.

'I thought we'd start,' the Professor announced, having coughed and cleared his throat, with the "Pathétique".' He fiddled with the record-player while everyone sat down, Ruth Cusper on the floor. He was a biggish man in a grey suit that faintly recalled the clothes of Woodward, Whipp and Woolmer-Mills. On a large head hair was still in plentiful supply even though the Professor was fifty-eight. The hair was grey also, bushing out around his head in a manner that suggested professorial vagueness rather than a gesture in the direction of current fashion. His wife, who stood by his side while he placed a record on the turntable, wore a magenta skirt and twin-set, and a string of jade beads. In almost every way – including this lively choice of dress – she seemed naturally to complement her husband, to fill the gaps his personality couldn't be bothered with. Her nervous manner was the opposite of his confident one. He gave his parties out of duty, and having done so found it hard to take an interest in any students except those who had already proved themselves academically sound. Mrs Skully preferred to strike a lighter note. Now and again she made efforts to entice a few of the girls to join her on Saturday evenings, offering the suggestion that they might listen together to Saturday Night Theatre and afterwards sit around and discuss it. Because the Professor saw no point in television there was none in the Skullys' house.

Tchaikovsky filled the sitting-room. The Professor sat down and then Mrs Skully did. The doorbell rang.

'Ah, of course,' Mrs Skully said.

'Valerie Upcott,' Valerie said. 'Good evening, Mrs Skully.'

'Come in, come in, dear. The "Pathétique's" just started.' She remarked in the hall on the green corduroy dress that was revealed when Valerie took off her coat. The green was of so dark a shade that it might almost have been black. It had large green buttons all down the front. 'Oh, how really nice!' Mrs Skully said.

The crackers that decorated the scenes of Hanover

looked sinister, Valerie thought: Christmas was on the way, soon there'd be the coloured lights and imitation snow. She smiled at Mrs Skully. She wondered about saying that her magenta outfit was nice also, but decided against it. 'We'll slip in quietly,' Mrs Skully said.

Valerie tried to forget the crackers as she entered the sitting-room and took her place on a chair, but in her mind the brash images remained. They did so while she acknowledged Kilroy's winking smile and while she glanced towards the Professor in case he chose to greet her. But the Professor, his head bent over clasped hands, did not look up.

Among the history students Valerie was an unknown quantity. During the two years they'd all known one another she'd established herself as a person who was particularly quiet. She had a private look even when she smiled, when the thin features of her face were startled out of tranquillity, as if an electric light had suddenly been turned on. Kilroy still tried to take her out, Ruth Cusper was pally. But Valerie's privacy, softened by her sudden smile, unfussily repelled these attentions.

For her part she was aware of the students' curiosity, and yet she could not have said to any one of them that a tragedy which had occurred was not properly in the past yet. She could not mention the tragedy to people who didn't know about it already. She couldn't tell it as a story because to her it didn't seem in the least like that. It was a fact you had to live with, half wanting to forget it, half feeling you could not. This time of year and the first faint signs of Christmas were enough to tease it brightly into life.

The second movement of the 'Pathétique' came to an end, the Professor rose to turn the record over, the students murmured. Mrs Skully slipped away, as she always did at this point, to attend to matters in the kitchen. While the Professor was bent over the record-player Kilroy waved his bottle of vodka about and then raised it to his lips. 'Hallo, Valerie,' Yvonne Smith whispered across the distance that separated them. She endeavoured to continue her communication by shaping words with her lips. Valerie smiled at her and at Ruth Cusper, who had turned her head when she'd heard Yvonne Smith's greeting. 'Hi,' Ruth Cusper said.

The music began again. The mouthing of Yvonne Smith continued for a moment and then ceased. Valerie didn't notice that, because in the room the students and the Professor were shadows of a kind, the music a distant piping. The swish of wind was in the room, and the shingle, cold on her bare feet; so were the two flat stones they'd placed on their clothes to keep them from blowing away. White flecks in the air were snow, she said: Christmas snow, what everyone wanted. But he said the flecks were flecks of foam.

He took her hand, dragging her a bit because the shingle hurt the soles of her feet and slowed her down. He hurried on the sand, calling back to her, reminding her that it was her idea, laughing at her hesitation. He called out something else as he ran into the breakers, but she couldn't hear because of the roar of the sea. She stood in the icy shallows and when she heard him shouting again she imagined he was still mocking her. She didn't even know he was struggling, she wasn't in the least aware of his death. It was his not being there she noticed, the feeling of being alone on the strand at Ballyquin.

'Cup, Miss Upcott?' the Professor offered in the dining-room. Poised above a glass, a jug contained a yellowish liquid. She said she'd rather have tea.

There were egg sandwiches and cakes, plates of crisps, biscuits and Twiglets. Mrs Skully poured tea, Ruth Cusper handed round the cups and saucers. The O'Neill sisters and their followers shared an obscene joke, which was a game that had grown up at the Skullys' parties: one student doing his best to make the others giggle too noisily. A point was gained if the Professor demanded to share the fun.

'Oh, but of course there isn't any argument,' Bewley Joal was insisting, still talking to Yvonne Smith about Moral Rearmament. Words had ceased to dribble from her lips. Instead she kept nodding her head. 'We live in times of decadence,' Bewley Joal pronounced.

Woodward, Whipp and Woolmer-Mills were still together, Woolmer-Mills launching himself endlessly on to the balls of his feet, Whipp sucking at his cheeks. No conversation was taking place among them: when the Professor finished going round with his jug of cup, talk of some kind would begin, probably about a mediaeval document Woodward had earlier mentioned. Or about a reference to *panni streit sine grano* which had puzzled Woolmer-Mills.

'Soon be Christmas,' Honor Hitchcock remarked to Valerie.

'Yes, it will.'

'I love it. I love the way you can imagine everyone doing just the same things on Christmas Eve, tying up presents, running around with holly, listening to the carols. And Christmas Day: that same meal in millions of houses, and the same prayers. All over the world.'

'Yes, there's that.'

'Oh, I think it's marvellous.'

'Christmas?' Kilroy said, suddenly beside them. He laughed, the fat on his face shaking a bit. 'Much overrated in my small view.' He glanced as he spoke at the Professor's profile, preparing himself in case the Professor should look in his direction. His expression changed, becoming solemn.

There were specks of what seemed like paint on a sleeve of the Professor's grey suit. She thought it odd that Mrs Skully hadn't drawn his attention to them. Valerie thought it odd that Kilroy was so determined about his Third. And that Yvonne Smith didn't just walk away from the clanking voice of Bewley Joal.

'Orange or coffee?' Ruth Cusper proffered two cakes that had been cut into slices. The fillings in Mrs Skully's cakes were famous, made with Trex and castor sugar. The cakes themselves had a flat appearance, like large biscuits.

'I wouldn't touch any of that stuff,' Kilroy advised, jocular again. 'I was up all night after it last year.'

'Oh, nonsense!' Ruth Cusper placed a slice of orange-cake on Valerie's plate, making a noise that indicated she found Kilroy's attempt at wit a failure. She passed on, and Kilroy without reason began to laugh.

Valerie looked at them, her eyes pausing on each face in the room. She was different from these people of her own age because of her autumn melancholy and the bitterness of Christmas. A solitude had been made for her, while they belonged to each other, separate yet part of a whole.

She thought about them, envying them their ordinary normality, the good fortune they accepted as their due. They trailed no horror, no ghosts or images that wouldn't go away: you could tell that by looking at them. Had she herself already been made peculiar by all of it, eccentric and strange and edgy? And would it never slip away, into the past where it belonged? Each year it was the same, no different from the year before, intent on hanging on to her. Each year she smiled and made an effort. She was brisk with it, she did her best. She told herself she had to live with it, agreeing with herself that of course she had to, as if wishing to be overheard. And yet to die so young, so pointlessly and so casually, seemed to be something you had to feel unhappy about. It dragged out tears from you; it made you hesitate again, standing in the icy water. Your idea it had been.

'Tea, you people?' Mrs Skully offered.

'Awfully kind of you, Mrs Skully,' Kilroy said. 'Splendid tea this is.'

'I should have thought you'd be keener on the Professor's cup, Mr Kilroy.'

'No, I'm not a cup man, Mrs Skully.'

Valerie wondered what it would be like to be Kilroy. She wondered about his private thoughts, even what he was thinking now as he said he wasn't a cup man. She imagined him in his bedroom, removing his royal-blue suit and meticulously placing it on a hanger, talking to himself about the party, wondering if he had done himself any damage in the Professor's eyes. She imagined him as a child, plump in bathing-trunks, building a sandcastle. She saw him in a kitchen, standing on a chair by an open cupboard, nibbling the corner of a crystallized orange.

She saw Ruth Cusper too, bossy at a children's party, friendlily bossy, towering over other children. She made them play a game and wasn't disappointed when they didn't like it. You couldn't hurt Ruth Cusper; she'd grown an extra skin beneath her motor-cycling gear. At night, she often said, she fell asleep as soon as her head touched the pillow.

You couldn't hurt Bewley Joal, either: a grasping child Valerie saw him as, watchful and charmless. Once he'd been hurt, she speculated: another child had told him that no one enjoyed playing with him, and he'd resolved from that moment not to care about stuff like that, to push his way through other people's opinion of him, not wishing to know it.

As children, the O'Neill sisters teased; their faithful tormentors pulled their hair. Woodward, Whipp and Woolmer-Mills read the *Children's Encyclopaedia*. Honor Hitchcock and the Reverend played mummies and daddies. 'Oh, listen to that chatterbox!' Yvonne Smith's father dotingly cried, affection that Yvonne Smith had missed ever since.

In the room the clanking of Bewley Joal punctuated the giggling in the corner where the O'Neill sisters were. More tea was poured and more of the Professor's cup, more cake was handed round. 'Ah, yes,' the Professor began. '*Panni streit sine grano.*' Woodward, Whipp and Woolmer-Mills bent their heads to listen.

The Professor, while waiting on his upstairs landing for Woolmer-Mills to use the lavatory, spoke of the tomatoes he grew. Similarly delayed downstairs, Mrs Skully suggested to the O'Neill sisters that they might like, one Saturday night next term, to listen to Saturday Night Theatre with her. It was something she enjoyed, she said, especially the discussion afterwards. 'Or you, Miss Upcott,' she said. 'You've never been to one of my evenings either.'

Valerie smiled politely, moving with Mrs Skully towards the sitting-room, where Tchaikovsky once more resounded powerfully. Again she examined the arrayed faces. Some eyes were closed in sleep, others were weary beneath a weight of tedium. Woodward's newt-like countenance had not altered, nor had Kilroy's fear dissipated. Frustration still tugged at Yvonne Smith.

47

Nothing much was happening in the face of Mrs Skully.

Valerie continued to regard Mrs Skully's face and suddenly she found herself shivering. How could that mouth open and close, issuing invitations without knowing they were the subject of derision? How could this woman, in her late middle age, officiate at student parties in magenta and jade, or bake inedible cakes without knowing it? How could she daily permit herself to be taken for granted by a man who cared only for students with academic success behind them? How could she have married his pomposity in the first place? There was something wrong with Mrs Skully, there was something missing, as if some part of her had never come to life. The more Valerie examined her the more extraordinary Mrs Skully seemed, and then it seemed extraordinary that the Professor should be unaware that no one liked his parties. It was as if some part of him hadn't come to life either, as if they lived together in the dead wood of a relationship, together in this house because it was convenient.

She wondered if the other students had ever thought that, or if they'd be bothered to survey in any way whatsoever the Professor and his wife. She wondered if they saw a reflection of the Skullys' marriage in the brownness of the room they all sat in, or in the crunchy fillings of Mrs Skully's cakes, or in the upholstered dining-chairs that were not comfortable. You couldn't blame them for not wanting to think about the Skullys' marriage: what good could come of it? The other students were busy and more organized than she. They had aims in life. They had futures she could sense, as she had sensed their pasts. Honor Hitchcock and the Reverend would settle down as right as rain in a provincial rectory, the followers of the O'Neill sisters would enter various business worlds. Woodward, Whipp and Woolmer-Mills would be the same as the Professor, dandruff on the shoulders of three grey suits. Bewley Joal would rise to heights, Kilroy would not. Ruth Cusper would run a hall of residence, the O'Neill sisters would give two husbands hell in Lurgan. Yvonne Smith would live in hopes.

The music of Tchaikovsky gushed over these reflections, as if to soften some harshness in them. But to Valerie there was no harshness in her contemplation of these people's lives, only fact and a lacing of speculation. The Skullys would go on ageing and he might never turn to his wife and say he was sorry. The O'Neill sisters would lose their beauty and Bewley Joal his vigour. One day Woolmer-Mills would find that he could no longer launch himself on to the balls of his feet. Kilroy would enter a home for the senile. Death would shatter the cotton-wool cosiness of Honor Hitchcock and the Reverend.

She wondered what would happen if she revealed what she had thought, if she told them that in order to keep her melancholy in control she had played about with their lives, seeing them in childhood, visiting them with old age and death. Which of them would seek to stop her while she cited the arrogance of the Professor and the pusillanimity of his wife? She heard her own voice echoing in a silence, telling them finally, in explanation, of the tragedy in her own life.

'Please all have a jolly Christmas,' Mrs Skully urged in the hall as scarves and coats were lifted from the hall-stand. 'Please now.'

'We shall endeavour,' Kilroy promised, and the others made similar remarks, wishing Mrs Skully a happy Christmas herself, thanking her and the Professor for the party, Kilroy adding that it had been most enjoyable. There'd be another, the Professor promised, in May.

There was the roar of Ruth Cusper's motor-cycle, and the overloading of Kilroy's Mini, and the striding into the night of Bewley Joal, and others making off on bicycles. Valerie walked with Yvonne Smith through the suburban roads. 'I quite like Joal,' Yvonne Smith confided, releasing the first burst of her pent-up chatter. 'He's all right, isn't he? Quite nice, really, quite clever. I mean, if you care for a clever kind of person. I mean, I wouldn't mind going out with him if he asked me.'

Valerie agreed that Bewley Joal was all right if you cared for that kind of person. It was pleasant in the cold night air. It was good that the party was over.

Yvonne Smith said good-night, still chattering about Bewley Joal as she turned into the house where her lodgings were. Valerie walked on alone, a thin shadow in the gloom. Compulsively now, she thought about the party, seeing again the face of Mrs Skully and the Professor's face and the faces of the others. They formed, like a backdrop in her mind, an assembly as vivid as the tragedy that more grimly visited it. They seemed like the other side of the tragedy, as if she had for the first time managed to peer round a corner. The feeling puzzled her. It was odd to be left with it after the Skullys' end-of-term party.

In the garden of the hall of residence the fallen leaves were sodden beneath her feet as she crossed a lawn to shorten her journey. The bewilderment she felt lifted a little. She had been wrong to imagine she envied other people their normality and good fortune. She was as she wished to be. She paused in faint moonlight, repeating that to herself and then repeating it again. She did not quite add that the tragedy had made her what she was, that without it she would not possess her reflective introspection, or be sensitive to more than just the time of year. But the thought hovered with her as she moved towards the lights of the house, offering what appeared to be a hint of comfort.

Cheating at Canasta

It was a Sunday evening; but Sunday, Mallory remembered, had always been as any other day at Harry's Bar. In the upstairs restaurant the waiters hurried with their loaded plates, calling out to one another above the noisy chatter. Turbot, *scaloppa alla Milanese*, grilled chops, scrambled eggs with bacon or smoked salmon, peas or *spinaci al burro*, mash done in a particularly delicious way: all were specialities here, where the waiters' most remarkable skill was their changing of the tablecloths with a sleight of hand that was admired a hundred times a night, and even occasionally applauded. Downstairs, Americans and Italians stood three or four deep at the bar and no one heard much of what anyone else said.

Bulky without being corpulent, sunburnt, blue-eyed, with the look of a weary traveller, Mallory was an Englishman in the middle years of his life and was, tonight, alone. Four of those years had passed since he had last sat down to dinner with his wife in Harry's Bar. 'You

promise me you'll go back for both of us,' Julia had
pleaded when she knew she would not be returning to
Venice herself, and he had promised; but more time
than he'd intended had slipped by before he had done
so. 'What was it called?' Julia had tried to remember,
and he said Harry's Bar.

The kir he'd asked for came. He ordered turbot, a
Caesar salad first. He pointed at a Gavi that had not been
on the wine list before. '*Perfetto!*' the waiter approved.

There was a pretence that Julia could still play cards,
and in a way she could. On his visits they would sit
together on the sofa in the drawing-room of her con-
finement and challenge one another in another game
of Canasta, which so often they had played on their
travels or in the garden of the house they'd lived in since
their marriage, where their children had been born. 'No
matter what,' Julia had said, aware then of what was
coming, 'let's always play cards.' And they did; for even
with her memory gone, a little more of it each day – her
children taken, her house, her flowerbeds, belongings,
clothes – their games in the communal drawing-room
were a reality her affliction still allowed. Not that there
was order in their games, not that they were games at
all; but still her face lit up when she found a joker or a
two among her cards, was pleased that she could do
what her visitor was doing, even though she couldn't

quite, even though once in a while she didn't know who he was. He picked up from the floor the Kings and Jacks, the eights and tens her fumbling fingers dropped. He put them to one side, it didn't matter where. He cheated at Canasta and she won.

The promise Julia had exacted from her husband had been her last insistence. Perturbation had already begun, a fringe of the greyness that was to claim her so early in her life. Because, tonight, he was alone where so often she had been with him, Mallory recalled with piercing rawness that request and his assent to it. He had not hesitated but had agreed immediately, wishing she had asked for something else. Would it have mattered much, he wondered in the crowded restaurant, if he had not at last made this journey, the first of the many she had wanted him to make? In the depths of her darkening twilight, if there still were places they belonged in a childhood he had not known, among shadows that were hers, not his, not theirs. In all that was forgotten how could it matter if a whim, forgotten too, was put aside, as the playing cards that fell from her hand were?

A table for six was lively in a corner, glasses raised; a birthday celebration it appeared to be. A couple who hadn't booked, or had come too early, were sent away. A tall, thin woman looked about her, searching for someone who wasn't there. The last time, Mallory remembered, their table had been by the door.

He went through the contents of his wallet: the familiar cards, the list of the telephone numbers he always brought abroad, some unused tickets for the Paris Métro, scraps of paper with nothing on them, coloured slips unnecessarily retained. Its *carte bancaire* stapled to it, the bill of his hotel in Paris was folded twice and was as bulky as his tidy wad of euro currency notes. *Lisa* someone had scribbled on the back of a fifty. His wine came.

He had travelled today from Monterosso, from the coast towns of the Cinque Terre, where often in September they had walked the mountain paths. The journey in the heat had been uncomfortable. He should have broken it, she would have said – a night in Milan, or Brescia to look again at the Foppas and the convent. Of course he should have arranged that, Mallory reflected, and felt foolish that he hadn't, and then foolish for being where he was, among people who were here for pleasure, or reasons more sensible than his. It was immediately a relief when a distraction came, his melancholy interrupted by a man's voice.

'Why are you crying?' an American somewhere asked.

This almost certainly came from the table closest to his own, but all Mallory could see when he slightly turned his head was a salt-cellar on the corner of a tablecloth. There was no response to the question that had been asked, or none that he heard, and the silence that gathered went on. He leaned back in his chair, as if wishing to glance more easily at a framed black-and-white photograph on the wall – a street scene dominated by a towering flat-iron block. From what this movement allowed, he established that the girl who had been asked why she was crying wasn't crying now. Nor was there a handkerchief clenched in the slender, fragile-seeming fingers on the tablecloth. A fork in her other hand played with the peas on her plate, pushing them about. She wasn't eating.

A dressed-up child too young even to be at the beginning of a marriage, but instinctively Mallory knew that she was already the wife of the man who sat across the table from her. A white band drew hair as smooth as ebony back from her forehead. Her dress, black too, was severe in the same way, unpatterned, its only decoration the loop of a necklace that matched the single pearl of each small earring. Her beauty startled Mallory – the delicacy of her features, her deep, unsmiling eyes – and he could tell that there was more of it, lost now in the empty gravity of her discontent.

'A better fellow than I am.' Her husband was ruddy, hair tidily brushed and parted, the knot of a red silk tie neither too small nor clumsily large in its crisp white collar, his linen suit uncreased. Laughing slightly when there was no response, either, to his statement about someone else being a better fellow, he added: 'I mean, the sort who gets up early.'

Mallory wondered if they were what he'd heard called Scott Fitzgerald people, and for a moment imagined he had wondered it aloud – as if, after all, Julia had again come to Venice with him. It was their stylishness, their deportment, the young wife's beauty, her silence going on, that suggested Scott Fitzgerald, a surface held in spite of an unhappiness. 'Oh but,' Julia said, 'he's careless of her feelings.'

'*Prego, signore.*' The arrival of Mallory's Caesar salad shattered this interference with the truth, more properly claiming his attention and causing him to abandon his pretence of an interest in something that wasn't there. It was a younger waiter who brought the salad, who might even be the boy – grown up a bit – whom Julia had called the *primo piatto* boy and had tried her Italian on. While Mallory heard himself wished *buon appetito*, while the oil and vinegar were placed more conveniently on the table, he considered that yes, there was a likeness, certainly of manner. It hadn't been understood by the boy at first when Julia asked him in Italian how long he'd been a waiter, but then he'd said he had begun at Harry's Bar only a few days ago and had been nowhere before. '*Subito, signore,*' he promised now when Mallory asked for pepper, and poured more wine before he went away.

'I didn't know Geoffrey got up early.' At the table that was out of sight her voice was soft, the quietness of its tone registering more clearly than what it conveyed. Her husband said he hadn't caught this. 'I didn't know he got up early,' she repeated.

'It's not important that he does. It doesn't matter what time the man gets up. I only said it to explain that he and I aren't in any way alike.'

'I know you're not like Geoffrey.'

'Why were you crying?'

Again there was no answer, no indistinct murmur, no lilt in which words were lost.

'You're tired.'

'Not really.'

'I keep not hearing what you're saying.'

'I said I wasn't tired.'

Mallory didn't believe she hadn't been heard: her husband was closer to her than he was and he'd heard the 'Not really' himself. The scratchy irritation nurtured malevolence unpredictably in both of them, making her not say why she had cried and causing him to lie. My God, Mallory thought, what they are wasting!

'No one's blaming you for being tired. No one can help being tired.'

She didn't take that up and there was silence while, again, the surface held and Mallory finished his Caesar salad. He was the only diner on his own in the upstairs restaurant, where for a moment on his arrival he had been faintly disappointed not to be recognized. He had recognized, himself, the features of the waiter who had led him to his table; there had later been that familiarity about the younger one; nor could he help remembering, from four years ago, the easy warmth of the welcome that had suggested stirrings of recognition then. But he hadn't been a man on his own four years ago, and naturally it was difficult for restaurant waiters when they were presented with only part of what there'd been before. And perhaps he was a little more crumpled than before; and four years was a longer lapse of time than there ever was in the past.

'My sister married Geoffrey,' the girl at the table behind him was saying.

'Yes, she did. And all I'm trying to say –'

'I know what you're saying.'

'It's just I wonder if you do.'

'You're saying I thought it would be like Geoffrey and Ellen. That I was looking forward to what isn't there.'

'It's hard to understand why anyone married Geoffrey.'

Tonight it didn't matter what they said. Dreary Geoffrey, who rose early to read his emails or scrutinize his bank statements, who liked to lead an ordered life, was enough tonight to nourish their need to punish one another. That her sister's marriage wasn't much was something to throw into their exchanges, to comment on tonight because it hadn't, perhaps, been touched upon before. 'Now, we don't know one single bit of that,' Julia in her occasionally stern way might have said, and seemed to say it now. 'Talk to me instead.'

He smiled. And across the restaurant a woman in the jolly birthday party waved at him – as if she thought he'd smiled at her, or imagined she must know him and couldn't place him, or just felt sorry for him, alone like that in such convivial surroundings. He nodded, not letting his smile go, then looked away. For all her moments of sternness, how often on their travels had Julia speculated as wildly as he ever had himself about people they didn't know! Lovers embracing in the Fauchon tea-rooms, the Japanese at the Uffizi, Germans in the Lido sun, or café-table chatterers anywhere. And they'd been listened to themselves, that stood to reason – he taken for a country doctor, Julia had maintained, and she an almoner or something like it. English both of them, of course, for anyone could tell, their voices confirmed as upper class when there'd been curiosity as to that.

'*Va bene?*' the waiter who'd been the *primo piatto* boy enquired, lifting away the Caesar-salad plate. 'Was fine?'

'*Va bene. Va bene.*'

'*Grazie, signore.*'

San Giovanni in Bragora was where the Cima *Baptism* they liked was: elusive on the train that morning and ever since, the name of the church came back. Sometimes when you looked it seemed that Christ was still in the shallow water, but looking again it wasn't so: the almost naked figure stood on dry land at the water's edge. The church of the Frari had Bellini's triptych; the saints he'd painted when he was over eighty were in San Giovanni Crisostomo. How could it make a difference, not going again, alone, to admire them? Or standing or not standing before the Vivarini *Annunciation* in San Giobbe and whatever there was in Madonna dell'Orto? She'd be asleep now. As early as five o'clock they were put to bed sometimes.

'I'm not,' the girl was saying. 'If we're telling the truth, I'm not.'

'No one can expect to be happy all the time.'

'You asked me. I'm telling you because you asked me.'

Their waiter brought them raspberries, with meringue and ice-cream. Mallory watched the confections going by and heard the murmurs of the husband.

'Why have we ordered this?' the girl complained when the waiter had gone.

'You wanted it.'

'Why did you say I should have married Geoffrey?'

'I didn't say –'

'Well, whatever.'

'Darling, you're tired.'

'Why did we come here?'

'Someone told us it was good.'

'Why did we come to Venice?'

It was his turn not to reply. Marriage was an uncalculated risk, Mallory remembered saying once. The trickiest of all undertakings, he might have called it, might even have suggested that knowing this was an insurance against the worst, a necessary awareness of what unwelcome surprises there might be. 'At least that's something,' Julia had agreed, and said she hoped it was enough. 'Love's cruel angels at play,' she called it when they upset one another.

The quiet at the other table went on. '*Grazie mille, signore*,' Mallory heard when eventually it was broken, the bill paid then. He heard the chairs pulled back and then the couple who had quarrelled passed close to

63

where he sat and on an impulse he looked up and spoke to them. He wondered as he did so if he had already had too much to drink, for it wasn't like him to importune strangers. He raised a hand in a gesture of farewell, hoping they would go on. But they hesitated, and he sensed their realization that he, who so clearly was not American, was English. There was a moment of disbelief, and then acceptance. This registered in their features, and shame crept in before the stylishness that had dissipated in the course of their quarrel returned to come to their rescue. His polite goodwill in wishing them good evening as they went by was politely acknowledged, smiles and pleasantness the harmless lies in their denial of all he'd heard. 'Its reputation's not exaggerated,' the husband commented with easy charm. 'It's good, this place.' Her chops had been delicious, she said.

Falling in with this, Mallory asked them if it was their first time in Venice. Embarrassment was still there, but they somehow managed to make it seem like their reproval of themselves for inflicting their bickering on him.

'Oh, very much so,' they said together, each seeming instinctively to know how their answer should be given.

'Not yours, I guess?' the husband added, and Mallory shook his head. He'd been coming to Venice since first he'd been able to afford it, he said. And then he told them why he was here alone.

While he did so Mallory sensed in his voice an echo of his regret that foolishness had brought him here. He did not say it. He did not say that he was here to honour a whim that would have been forgotten as soon as it was expressed. He did not deplore a tiresome, futile journey. But he'd come close to doing so and felt ashamed in turn. His manner had dismissed the scratchiness he'd eavesdropped on as the unseemly stuff of marriage. It was more difficult to dismiss his own sly aberration, and shame still nagged.

'I'm sorry about your wife.' The girl's smile was gentle. 'I'm very sorry.'

'Ah, well.' Belittling melancholy, he shook his head.

Again the playing cards fall. Again he picks them up. She wins and then is happy, not knowing why.

The party at the corner table came to an end, its chatter louder, then subdued. A handbag left behind was rescued by a waiter. Other people came.

Tomorrow what has been lost in recollection's collapse will be restored as she has known it: the pink and gold of Sant Giobbe's *Annunciation*, its dove, its Virgin's features, its little trees, its God. Tomorrow the silenced music will play in the piazza of San Marco, and tourists shuffle in the *calles*, and the boats go out to the islands. Tomorrow the cats of Venice will be fed by ladies in the dried-out parks, and there'll be coffee on the Zattere.

'No, no,' he murmured when the husband said he was sorry too. 'No, no.'

He watched the couple go, and smiled across the crowded restaurant when they reached the door. Shame isn't bad, her voice from somewhere else insists. Nor the humility that is its gift.

a little history

Penguin Modern Classics were launched in 1961, and have been shaping the reading habits of generations ever since.

The list began with distinctive grey spines and evocative pictorial covers – a look that, after various incarnations, continues to influence their current design – and with books that are still considered landmark classics today.

Penguin Modern Classics have caused scandal and political change, inspired great films and broken down barriers, whether social, sexual or the boundaries of language itself. They remain the most provocative, groundbreaking, exciting and revolutionary works of the last 100 years (or so).

In 2011, on the fiftieth anniversary of the Modern Classics, we're publishing fifty Mini Modern Classics: the very best short fiction by writers ranging from Beckett to Conrad, Nabokov to Saki, Updike to Wodehouse. Though they don't take long to read, they'll stay with you long after you turn the final page.

 MODERN CLASSICS
www.penguinclassics.com